THE DARK REALM

KAYMON
THE GORGON
HOUND

With special thanks to Allan Frewin Jones

*For Joseph Lawrence Robert
Smithers Shepherd*

www.beastquest.co.uk

ORCHARD BOOKS
338 Euston Road, London NW1 3BH
Orchard Books Australia
Level 17/207 Kent St, Sydney, NSW 2000

A Paperback Original
First published in Great Britain in 2008

Beast Quest is a registered trademark of Working Partners Limited
Series created by Working Partners Limited, London

Text © Working Partners Limited 2008
Cover illustration by Steve Sims © Orchard Books 2008
Inside illustrations by Brian@KJA-artists.com © Orchard Books 2008

A CIP catalogue record for this book is available from
the British Library.

ISBN 978 1 40830 001 5

10

Printed in Great Britain by J F Print Ltd.,
Sparkford, Somerset

The paper and board used in this paperback are natural recyclable
products made from wood grown in sustainable forests. The
manufacturing processes conform to the environmental regulations
of the country of origin.

Orchard Books is a division of Hachette Children's Books,
an Hachette UK company

www.hachette.co.uk

KAYMON
THE GORGON
HOUND

BY ADAM BLADE

ORCHARD BOOKS

Welcome. You stand on the edge of darkness, at the gates of an awful land. This place is Gorgonia, the Dark Realm, where the sky is red, the water black and Malvel rules. Tom and Elenna – your hero and his companion – must travel here to complete the next Beast Quest.

Gorgonia is home to six of the deadliest Beasts imaginable – minotaur, winged stallion, sea monster, Gorgon hound, mighty mammoth and scorpion man. Nothing can prepare Tom and Elenna for what they are about to face. Their past victories mean nothing. Only strong hearts and determination will save them now.

Dare you follow Tom's path once more? I advise you to turn back. Heroes can be stubborn and adventures may beckon, but if you decide to stay with Tom, you must be brave and fearless. Anything less will mean certain doom.

Watch where you step...

Kerlo the Gatekeeper

PROLOGUE

It was dark as the injured rebel limped away from the castle on the moor. He had used a smuggled metal file to saw through his manacles, and the jagged edge had slipped and cut into his skin. The pain in his ankle burned, but he was desperate to get away from that terrible place.

He thought of his fellow rebels languishing in the castle dungeons. Many of them had planned to escape with him, but it seemed he had been the only one to make it over the drawbridge. He threw himself under a gorse bush, gasping for breath.

"I need to rest," he muttered to himself.

After a while he crawled out and cautiously lifted his head. He frowned. A thick grey fog was sweeping across the moor like a ghostly tide, drowning the hills and valleys. The fog would make it harder for the soldiers to find him. But it would also make it difficult for him to see the prearranged signal lights of the rebels' friends.

The man stood up, staring blindly into the fog. Where were the lights?

Wait! He narrowed his eyes, peering into the distance. Then his heart leaped. He could see two yellow dots of light, blurred by the fog. The signal!

He stumbled forwards on his bleeding feet. Rescue was near. The lights were growing larger now, as if the bearers of lanterns were moving towards him. Two men, he assumed, walking side by side.

"Freedom or death!" he called. It was the agreed password.

He paused, listening for the response. But all he heard was a low moan that echoed through the fog.

He shivered, frowning again. Then he called the password once more.

The two lights began moving swiftly towards him. But although they rose and fell in a strange loping manner, they always kept exactly the same distance apart. A second low moan rumbled through the fog, and

this time there was another noise –
the unmistakable sound of large
teeth snapping.

Suddenly, something huge came
hurtling towards him out of the fog.

The man let out a cry, throwing up his arms to protect his face. Through his fingers, he saw the salivating fangs and ferocious yellow eyes of an enormous hound. The lights he'd seen were the Beast's glowing eyes!

A moment later, the snarling creature was upon him, throwing him onto his back, its savage claws ripping at his chest and face…

CHAPTER ONE

DEADLY FLOWERS

Tom and Elenna stood in the prow
of their boat as they returned to the
shore of the Black Ocean. With
the defeat of Narga the sea monster,
another good Beast of Avantia had
been freed – Sepron the sea serpent.
The two friends leaped down onto
the shingle, eager to be reunited with
their animal companions. Silver the
wolf let out a howl of delight, and

Storm, Tom's black stallion, reared up, neighing triumphantly.

Tom and Elenna already knew that another Quest lay ahead. Wizard Aduro, their friend and mentor, had briefly appeared on the ocean waves, warning them that they would soon face another evil Beast: Kaymon. But he hadn't given them any more details.

Tom touched the blue jewel from Narga's tooth, which he had won in his last fight against the sea monster. He had placed it in his magic belt next to the red jewel, which gave him the ability to understand the good Beasts, and the green jewel, with its power to heal broken bones. This new jewel gave him a knife-sharp memory. When he touched it, he remembered all the battles he had won in his Quest to rid Avantia of the Dark Wizard Malvel.

"Tom, look!" said Elenna. Tom turned and saw that his companion was studying the greasy, foul-smelling map of Gorgonia that Malvel had given them. She was pointing to a tiny picture of Nanook the snow monster that had appeared on the map.

Tom felt a sharp tingling in his shield. The bell of the snow monster, embedded there with the tokens of the other five good Beasts, was quivering.

Tom looked back at the map and the little image of Nanook. "Don't worry, my friend," he said. "We'll save you!"

"It looks as though she's being held captive somewhere in the south of Gorgonia," Elenna said. "But what kind of Beast could take her prisoner? She's one of the strongest of the good Beasts."

"Aduro said Kaymon was more evil than we could possibly imagine," Tom warned her.

"But what can that mean?" Elenna wondered.

"I think it's time we found out," Tom replied. The thought of Nanook being held prisoner burned his heart. "Come on, Storm – we have work to do!"

He leaped into the saddle and extended an arm to help Elenna up behind him.

"To the south!" Tom cried. "Let's rescue Nanook!"

The noble stallion galloped beneath the seething red Gorgonian skies, Silver at his side. Tom shivered, looking up at the red clouds that rolled and swirled above their heads. He would never get used to this terrible land!

"Don't forget to avoid the quicksand we wandered into before," Elenna said.

Tom nodded. "I remember it perfectly," he told her. "In fact, I can remember every hill and valley of this part of Gorgonia, thanks to Narga's jewel."

"That's good," Elenna said. "Especially as we can't completely trust Malvel's map. Remember the trouble it got us into last time?"

Soon the Black Ocean was far behind them and the sun was low on the horizon. They entered a grim landscape of broken hills.

"Have you noticed that it's getting

much hotter?" Tom said, wiping sweat from his forehead. "It must be terrible for Nanook to be imprisoned here." The snow monster was used to Avantia's northern ice fields, her thick white fur protecting her from bitter winter winds.

As they reached the top of the first hill, they found themselves staring into a wide valley filled with gigantic bluebells.

"Oh, how beautiful!" Elenna said. "I would never have expected to find such lovely flowers in a place like this." She frowned. "But what's that shape in the middle? I can't make it out."

Tom peered across the valley. Although the precious suit of golden armour had been returned to Avantia, he still possessed its magical powers,

and the armour's helmet allowed him
to see far into the distance.

"It's Nanook!" he said. "The poor
Beast is chained to a rock!"

Although shackled to a huge
lump of amber, Nanook still looked
majestic, her thick white fur glowing
under the red clouds. But she was
wrenching and tearing at the chain,
clearly in great distress.

"That's so cruel!" cried Elenna. "How could anyone cause her so much pain?" She leaped from the saddle and began to run down the hillside. Silver bounded beside her as she headed towards the blue sea of flowers.

"Be careful!" Tom called, urging Storm down the slope after them. He wasn't at all sure about the huge flowers, which had turned towards Elenna, almost as if they knew she was approaching.

"Wait!" Tom shouted, as Elenna and Silver waded into the waist-high stems.

A moment later Elenna stopped and began beating at the flowers with her hands.

"Tom! Help!" she shouted.

At her side, Silver was leaping back

and forth, howling and snarling as though he were being attacked by an invisible enemy.

Tom could see what was happening. The dark red stamens of the flowers were stabbing like daggers, hemming Elenna and Silver in with their needle-sharp blades. Silver was yelping in pain.

"Ouch!" Elenna cried. "Tom – it really hurts."

Tom pulled on the reins and brought Storm to a halt. He swung down from the saddle. There was only one thing he could do. Gripping his shield, Tom drew his sword and swung his blade through the vicious flowers, cutting a path towards his friends.

The flowers stabbed at him as he hacked through. He felt pain as sharp

as wasp stings as he sliced into the
stems. Using the speed given to him
by the golden leg armour, he quickly
reached Elenna and the wolf.

"Come on!" Tom called, alarmed to
see that the bluebells were swarming
behind him, lunging forwards to fill
the gap that he had made.

Elenna and Silver raced along with Tom close behind. The bluebells writhed all around, striking at them like snakes. At last they came diving out of the flowers, skidding in the dust as they reached safety.

Tom stared out over the bluebells. Nanook was still in the centre of the flowers, looking towards him in desperation. She lifted her arms and rattled her chain in anguish.

"The evil flowers are all around her," Tom said. "How will we ever be able to reach her?"

Then a low, mournful howl came echoing across the valley.

Tom and Elenna looked at one another.

"What was that?" Elenna asked.

Tom gripped his sword firmly. "Kaymon!" he said.

CHAPTER TWO

KAYMON'S POWER

The eerie howl rang out again.

"It sounds so lonely," Elenna
murmured, her voice trembling.

"But it sounds evil, too," Tom said,
as a third howl drifted on the wind.
"Look!" He pointed to a dark shape
on the hilltops to the west,
silhouetted against the blood-red disc
of the setting sun. With his extra-
keen vision, Tom could see a pair of

terrible yellow eyes that shone with a wicked light.

"It's a hound, Elenna!" he said.

A moment later, Kaymon came leaping down the hilltop, still some distance away but hurtling rapidly towards them with gnashing, slavering fangs. Soon she was crashing through the blue flowers. Her teeth ripped their heads off and her huge feet crushed them as she tore a path towards Tom and his companions.

Storm tossed his head, his eyes rolling, as the hound drew rapidly closer. The fur bristled all along Silver's grizzled back and he growled, pawing the ground.

Kaymon was as large as a bull and her thick black fur was tangled and caked with filth. She gave off a

smell, too – a foul, choking stench
that made Tom reel.

As the Beast pounded forwards,
Tom saw the evil light in her eyes and
the terrible strength of her shoulders
and flanks. He also noticed something
else – the Beast wore a thick collar of
twisted gold around her neck, and set
deep into the precious metal was a
huge white jewel.

Tom caught hold of Storm's reins and stepped in front of Elenna, drawing his sword.

"Keep back!" he said to his friends, and waited, sword in hand, as the hound came crashing out of the flowers.

Suddenly, Silver jumped past him, his teeth bared as he sprang at the Beast's throat.

"Silver, no!" Tom shouted.

But the wolf ignored his cries. Leaping high with his jaws wide, he sank his teeth into Kaymon's neck.

The hound snarled and howled, shaking her head as she tried to free herself. But Silver's jaws held her in a deadly grip, his claws tearing at the Beast's fur.

For a few moments Silver put up a tremendous fight. But then Kaymon let out a ferocious roar and her whole body suddenly began to swell, writhing and distorting and changing shape so that Silver lost his grip and was thrown off.

"What's happening?" Elenna cried.

"She's changing!" Tom shouted in horror.

Instead of one hound, there were now three!

Tom stared in disbelief, his heart almost stopping in his chest. Each of the Beasts was as huge and as savage as the first, and all three turned on

Silver as he stood panting and snarling.

"He doesn't stand a chance!" Elenna cried as the hounds leaped on the startled wolf.

Silver vanished from sight under the dark bulk of their powerful bodies, his angry growls drowned out by the snapping and snarling of the three hounds.

Tom turned to Elenna. "Take Storm's reins," he said urgently. "I have to rescue Silver!" He tightened his grip on his shield and brandished his sword as he ran forwards.

One of the hounds turned from the wolf, its yellow eyes blazing. A moment later it was in the air, leaping at Tom's head.

"Watch out!" he heard Elenna shout.

Tom lifted his shield to deflect the
sharp claws that were reaching out to
gouge his eyes. The weight of the
hound sent him staggering backwards
and he almost fell, but he managed
to hold his ground, digging in his
heels. Using the strength given to
him by the golden breastplate, he
blocked the hound's charge with his

shield and sent it crashing to one side. Then, with a sharp twist of his wrist, his sword pierced the hound's thick fur. Dark blood spurted from the wound as the Beast yelped in pain and turned tail, running away into the dusk.

Tom saw a second hound racing towards Elenna and Storm. Swift as lightning, Elenna fitted an arrow to her bow and let it fly. She loosed three arrows into the Beast, one after the other, as it hurtled towards her. The third arrow embedded itself deep in the hound's leg. Howling wildly, the evil creature twisted around, trying to bite at it.

"Well done!" Tom shouted, running towards his friends. The wounded Beast came to a tumbling halt, then it too raced away, snarling with pain. They had beaten two of the evil Beasts!

But the third hound was standing over Silver. The wolf lay on the ground, dreadfully still. Tom's heart was in his mouth. Was Silver already dead?

"No!" Tom yelled, running swiftly towards the third hound, his sword flashing.

Kaymon turned, her massive jaws opening and her eyes burning with a ferocious evil.

For a moment Tom and the Beast looked into one another's eyes. Then Tom raised his sword, aiming to plunge it into the monster's heart. But the hound turned and raced away through the sea of flowers, following the other two fleeing Beasts towards the distant hills.

"Come back and fight!" Tom shouted after them. He ran into the bluebells, beating the darting stamens back with his shield, determined to follow the escaping Beasts.

But a whimper from Silver stopped him. He paused, looking over his shoulder to where the wolf lay on the ground. Elenna knelt at Silver's side, cradling the wolf's head in her lap. Storm stood over them, whinnying anxiously.

Silver was badly injured, his flesh torn open all along his neck and flanks, his fur matted and blood-soaked from the claws and fangs of the three evil hounds.

"I can't leave Silver like this!" Tom murmured. But before going to the wolf he lifted his sword and shouted, "No matter how far you run, Kaymon, we will meet again. I promise!"

CHAPTER THREE

THE BINDING CHAIN

Silver lay panting with quick, shallow breaths, his eyes rolling back and his tongue lolling. Tom shuddered as he looked at the wolf's bloody wounds. Some of his ribs seemed broken.

Elenna wept, gently stroking Silver's neck, her tears mingling with the blood on his fur. "Can you save him, Tom?"

"I still have Epos's healing token, as

well as the green jewel," Tom told her. "I'm sure they'll be powerful enough to make Silver well again."

Tom hoped he sounded more confident than he felt. The healing token and the jewel had only previously been used on himself and on the good Beasts – he had no way of knowing if they would work on Silver.

He knelt at the wolf's side, taking the flame bird's talon from his shield and the jewel from his belt. He touched them against the worst of Silver's wounds – a hideous gash on his side and the broken ribs.

Tom felt a sudden surge of energy and pulses of red and green light flashed through his fingers as the healing power of the two tokens began to work together.

"His ribs are mending," Tom whispered. "Look!"

The arc of Silver's ribs was returning and the wounds were closing, the blood around them disappearing.

"Yes, I can see!" Elenna gasped, wiping the tears from her eyes. "Tom – that's wonderful!"

The energy sent a tingling power up Tom's arm as he watched the broken ribs knit together under Silver's flesh. In a few more moments the grey fur grew thickly again over the healed wounds. But the poor wolf was still weak and exhausted from his ordeal.

Tom stood up, staring out across the sea of blue flowers to where Nanook was still held captive, chained to the amber rock. The light was fading rapidly now, the amber glowing in the dusk. Now that Silver was better, it was time for Tom to act! There wasn't a moment to waste.

He took several steps back. Gathering all his strength, he ran and, at the very edge of the bluebells, leaped up into air, harnessing the power of the golden boots, as the flowers snapped at his heels.

"Oh, yes!" he shouted in excitement as he soared through the air, stretching out his legs for the landing. He knew it was going to be close...

But even such a great leap was not enough to clear the flowers. He landed near Nanook's clearing, but right among the deadly blooms. The red stamens stabbed at him. Using his shield to ward them off, he strode towards the snow monster, hacking at the bluebells with his sword.

Nanook roared and surged forwards to greet him, her long shaggy arms open. Tom sensed the good Beast's joy and relief as he stepped into the clearing. But the chain jerked her back and her face crumpled with pain and anger as she tugged at the heavy iron links that held her captive. Tom could see great sores where the chain had been rubbing his friend's skin.

"I'll set you free!" he promised.

Nanook grunted and snorted as Tom inspected the shackles. Each link was as thick as his wrist and the heavy chain was attached to the rock by great iron staples, driven deep into the amber.

"I'm going to cut the chain with my

sword," Tom told the snow monster.
He picked up a length of chain and
hung it over part of the amber rock.
Taking a deep breath he stepped
back. He lifted his sword above his
head with both hands and brought it
crashing down onto the iron links.
Clang! Tom's arms shivered to the
shoulder with the impact. But
the chain held.

He could faintly hear Elenna
shouting, "Come on, Tom! You can
do it!"

Gritting his teeth, Tom lifted his
sword again.

He brought the blade down with all
his might. There was an echoing
crack and a glow of amber light, then
the chain broke apart!

Nanook rose up onto her back legs
and gave a roar of delight while

Tom held his sword above his head in triumph.

Now they needed to get back to where Elenna and the others were waiting. Tom couldn't just jump across the flowers and leave Nanook behind. They had to do this together.

He started hacking at the flowers to cut a path through to his companions. Then Nanook scooped Tom up in her great arms and perched him high on her shoulder. He clung to her fur as she began to make her way through the bluebells.

"Thanks, Nanook!" he said, laughing.

The blue heads turned and the stamens stabbed viciously, but Nanook's fur was too thick for their evil blades. She ploughed onwards, crushing the flowers beneath her

huge feet. At last they made it
through the valley and were reunited
with Tom's friends.

Nanook was free! But Tom knew
that was not enough.

"Kaymon's still out there," he said.

"Our next task is to find her and defeat her." He looked at Elenna. "I need the white jewel from her collar for my belt. And unless she's defeated, we won't be able to get Nanook home."

The Quest was far from over.

CHAPTER FOUR

THE BEAST ON
THE BATTLEMENTS

Night had fallen, and the Gorgonian
sky was gloomy and starless.

"We will find a way to get you back
to Avantia," Tom vowed to Nanook.
"But Elenna and I need to defeat
Kaymon first." He hoped the snow
monster would understand what he
was saying, and concentrated on the
red jewel in his belt, knowing it
would help him to communicate

with her. "Will you stay here and protect Silver and Storm while we are gone?"

The good Beast frowned, then her eyes gleamed with comprehension and she grunted and nodded, one large hand reaching out to rest on Storm's neck, the other gently stroking Silver's fur as he lay beside her.

"Why do you want to leave Storm behind?" Elenna asked in a soft voice. "He would surely be useful to us on the hunt."

"There are three hounds out there," Tom said. "We can't take Silver with us in his condition, and I want three pairs of eyes watching out in case one of the Beasts comes back while we are gone."

Elenna looked at him uneasily.

"But that means we will only have two pairs of eyes watching out for us," she murmured.

"I know that," Tom said. "But we also have a magic shield and the powers from the golden armour." He smiled grimly. "And we have ourselves!" He put his hand on Elenna's shoulder. "We can do this," he said. "While there's blood in my veins, I will finish this Quest!"

An excited light sparkled in Elenna's eyes. "So will I!" she said.

Tom looked up into the bleak night sky. "We should sleep now," he said. "We can take it in turns to keep watch for Kaymon. And then, at first light, the Quest continues!"

As the red sun rose over the hills the next morning, Tom was already on his feet. Elenna took a few moments to bid farewell to Silver. The wolf was still very weak, but he licked Elenna's face gratefully.

"Are you sure you want to leave him?" Tom asked. "I can do this alone, if I need to."

"No!" Elenna said fiercely. "Kaymon hurt Silver. I'm going with you to find her!"

Tom said goodbye to Nanook and the animals, then the two friends headed off in pursuit of the Gorgon hound.

"We can circle the bluebells and pick up Kaymon's trail on the far side of the valley," Tom said.

There they saw three sets of large paw marks that led up the hillside and across the rugged landscape. The hills were jagged and sharp-edged, like rows of broken teeth.

A few bare plants grew among the rocks, every twig armed with a razor-sharp thorn.

After a while Tom noticed that the three sets of markings were closer together. Suddenly they merged into a single, much heavier trail.

"The hounds joined together again here," Tom said. "Kaymon must only split into three when she's in danger."

Soon Tom and Elenna crested a hill and found themselves staring at a dark castle standing on a mound in the middle of a bleak moor.

Elenna opened the map. "There's no castle shown here," she said.

Tom stared out across the moor, his keen vision bringing the gloomy fortress into sharp focus. It was surrounded by a moat of murky green water. Tom narrowed his eyes. The towering granite walls looked as though they contained dreadful secrets.

"I don't like the look of it," Elenna said with a shudder.

Tom's eyes rose to the jagged battlements. Something was moving up there.

"I can see Kaymon!" he said.

Pacing back and forth, high on the castle's turrets, her tail swinging, was the great hound. Then she stood still and turned towards Tom and Elenna, her yellow eyes burning. A moment later, her wide jaws opened and a terrible howl echoed out across the moor.

"She's seen us," Elenna said.

Tom drew his sword. "Then we shouldn't keep her waiting!" he said.

CHAPTER FIVE

THE EVIL CASTLE

Tom and Elenna ran through the
long grass of the moor, zigzagging as
they approached the castle. They
darted between mounds and low
hills, hoping that Kaymon would lose
sight of them. Finally, they arrived at
a ditch, where they lay to catch their
breaths. They were halfway to the
castle now. It towered up, pitch black
against the swirling red sky.

"The drawbridge is down," Tom said to Elenna, as he peered out of the ditch. "And the gate is open. There's no sign of any people and there aren't any lights. Perhaps the castle is abandoned?"

"We can't be sure of that," Elenna said.

"I know," Tom replied. He felt uneasy. "But we have to go in there."

"Can you see Kaymon?" Elenna asked.

"No. Not from here." Tom summoned his courage. "Come on!"

They raced towards the castle, crouching low, and began to cross the drawbridge. The wooden boards groaned underneath them, and as Tom came to the middle, the rotting timbers cracked under his feet. He drew back as a piece of

58

wood fell down into the stinking, weed-choked waters of the moat, leaving a ragged hole.

"Be careful," he said to Elenna. "The drawbridge is falling to pieces!"

They moved forwards, testing each step before putting their weight on the decayed wooden boards.

Tom looked around as they entered the gateway. The stones were slimy. Foul-smelling water oozed and dripped all around them. They stepped into a courtyard. The castle was totally silent. Doors hung open on their hinges, revealing glimpses of rooms where the furniture was overturned as though people had left in a panic.

"What do you think happened here?" Elenna asked, looking around anxiously. "Where is everyone?"

"Perhaps Kaymon chased them away," Tom suggested. He looked up towards the battlements. There was no sign of the evil Beast.

"Where is she?" Elenna asked.

"That's what I want to know," Tom said. "We have to find her before she finds us!" He held his sword out in front of him as he moved around the courtyard, kicking doors open as he searched for the Beast.

"Stay back," he warned Elenna. "But keep an arrow on your bow and be ready to fire the moment the Beast appears."

They made their way into one of the rooms. Open doors led into yet more rooms, but still they found nothing.

"Perhaps she's gone?" Elenna murmured.

"I doubt it," Tom replied. "She's ready for a fight."

The faintest of sounds came up from beneath the floorboards.

"Was that a voice?" Elenna asked, her eyes wide.

Tom took a deep breath. "Hello!" he shouted. "Is anyone there?"

They strained their ears, hardly

breathing. The sound came again, and this time there was no doubt – human voices were echoing up from deep beneath their feet.

At the same moment, a deep-throated howl boomed through the castle. Tom frowned, striding out into the courtyard. High on the battlements above the gatehouse, pacing slowly along the wall, was Kaymon. Tom's fingers closed around the hilt of his sword.

Then he noticed a movement in the shadows. A tall, bald-headed man emerged into the light. His clothes were ragged and he held a staff of gnarled wood. A patch covered one eye.

"Kerlo!" Tom gasped, recognising the gatekeeper who had greeted him when he first entered Gorgonia.

The man leaned on his staff, watching Tom keenly with his one eye. "It sounds as though someone needs help," he commented.

Elenna appeared at the doorway. She looked at the gatekeeper for a moment then turned to Tom. "The voices are getting louder," she said. "They sound desperate."

Tom stared up at Kaymon, who was still pacing. Then he drew his sword and followed Elenna inside. He would tackle the hound later. First he had to rescue the captives trapped in the castle's dark heart.

CHAPTER SIX

THE DUNGEONS

Tom and Elenna ran, looking for a way into the lower regions of the castle.

They pushed through a creaking door and came into a long corridor with dank walls lit by flaming torches.

"What was Kerlo doing here?" Elenna asked. "I feel as if he's on our side, although I can never be sure."

"I know what you mean," Tom

replied. "I don't always understand what he says, but I'm almost certain he's not our enemy."

They passed several doorways, but these only led to other deserted rooms. Winding stairways soon brought them deep under the ground. The air was stale and musty and rats scuttled about.

"This place is huge," Elenna said. "How will we ever find the captives?"

"We must!" Tom insisted. "Let's listen!"

They stood in a cobwebbed stone corridor, holding their breath, and heard the clamour of trapped people beneath them.

A single voice rose above the others. "Help us! Please help us!"

Tom stared at a ragged tapestry that hung on the wall. Its threadbare edge twitched as if disturbed by a breath of wind.

Tom strode over and pulled the cloth aside, revealing an arched doorway. It led to another stone stairway that wound downwards, its walls lit by smoking torches.

Tom looked at Elenna. "This is the way!" He took a torch from the wall and together they moved down into the gloom of the castle's deepest cellars.

Tom shuddered at the sight of the grimy, stinking dungeons. The walls were running with damp and patches of fungus clung to the stones, glowing with a sickly light. Clumps of sticky spiders' webs stuck to their clothing as they brushed past.

"This is terrible," Elenna whispered, her voice full of dread.

The voices grew louder. "We're here! Help us!"

Tom turned a corner and at last he saw the prisoners. There were about a dozen men in a filthy chamber, their limbs shackled in rusting chains and their clothes in tatters.

The prisoners pulled against their fetters. "Help us! Free us!" they called out.

Tom and Elenna ran forwards, taking out their water flasks and giving the men a drink.

"Who are you?" Tom asked.

One man, taller and broader than the others, got to his feet, his chains rattling in the iron ring that held them to the wall.

"We are Gorgonian rebels," he said. "Have you come over the moor? Did you see any of our comrades out there?"

Tom shook his head. "I'm sorry," he said. "I didn't see anyone."

"Please free us," the man said.

Tom looked at the manacles. The iron was rusted and old. "Keep still!" he warned the man, taking out his

sword and thrusting the tip into the
locking mechanism. He gave it a
sharp twist. The blade slipped and
grazed the man's skin. He hissed
with pain.

"I'm sorry," Tom gasped. "I'll try
that again."

He really needed to concentrate!

He pressed the tip of his sword to
the manacles a second time. The man

watched him anxiously. He turned the blade again and this time the iron shackle snapped open.

"Thank you," the man said. "If you could free my men we will be gone from here."

It wasn't long before all the rebels had been released from their chains. They stood up, rubbing their numbed limbs, smiling with gratitude and relief.

"Who are you?" the tall man asked, resting his hand on Tom's shoulder and looking sharply at Elenna.

"We come from another land," Tom said. "We're the friends of a good wizard." He wasn't sure how much he should tell these people.

"You have aided the rebellion!" the man said. "Thank you! But tell no one that you ever saw us. Malvel must not get to hear of this!"

Tom shivered at the mention of the evil wizard's name. "Malvel will hear nothing from us," he said. "Can we do anything else to help?" He felt sure that anyone rebelling against Malvel must be good.

"You have done enough," the man said. "But remember: never speak of this encounter!" He led his men out of the dungeon and soon they were gone.

The gatekeeper suddenly stepped from the shadows.

"Was that wise?" Kerlo asked, his one keen eye on Tom's face. Tom stared at him, troubled by a moment of doubt.

"They were starving," Elenna said.

"We had to let them go."

Kerlo's piercing eye turned to her. "Did you, indeed?" he growled. "Do you know what deeds these men are capable of?"

Tom looked at the gatekeeper, uncertainty creeping into his mind. Had they been right to set the men free? "They are against Malvel. They're on the same side as us – aren't they?" he asked.

But Kerlo just turned and walked slowly up the stairway without replying.

Tom was about to mount the stairs after him when the flickering light of his torch shone on something crammed into a crevice in the entrance to the stairway.

He moved the torch closer. It was a folded scrap of linen. He pulled it free.

Elenna leaned over his shoulder as he carefully opened it.

"What is it?" she asked.

"It's a lock of hair," Tom said in surprise. "And a piece of red silk."

Elenna let out a gasp. She picked up the lock of chestnut hair and held it against Tom's head. "It's exactly the same colour as yours!" she whispered.

Bewildered, Tom picked up the scrap of scarlet silk. "There's something embroidered on it," he murmured. "Elenna – hold it for me so I can shine the light on it."

Elenna stretched the silk between her fingers. It was a curling script, sewn onto the silk with fine yellow thread.

"Midsummer's Eve," Tom read. "But…but that's my birthday!"

The two friends looked at one another.

"Could it have been left here by your lost father?" Elenna asked.

Tom had never seen his father, Taladon, who had disappeared when Tom was a baby.

"Do you think he may have been here?" his friend continued.

Tom stared again at the piece of

silk. To think that his father might have stood in this very spot! For a moment, he felt closer to Taladon than he ever had before. His hand closed around the scrap.

"Come on, Elenna," he said. "My father would want me to do the right thing. We have an evil Beast to defeat."

Tom raced up the stone stairs. He was ready to bring this Quest to an end!

CHAPTER SEVEN

DEFEAT!

A deep-throated howl echoed down the stairwell.

"Kaymon!" gasped Elenna. "She sounds close!"

"She must have come down from the battlements," Tom said, pushing the linen rag and its mysterious contents into his tunic.

He raced up the stairs, groping in his pocket for the magical compass his father had left him. The needle could point to *Danger* or *Destiny* to help Tom make vital decisions. He took it out as he ran along the corridor and saw that the needle was wavering.

There was no sign of the rebels. Tom guessed that they must have left the castle.

He heard Elenna right behind him as he ran back into the room that led to the courtyard. Beyond the open door, he could see the huge shape of Kaymon moving restlessly to and fro, waiting for Tom.

Tom looked at the compass again. Now the needle pointed firmly to *Destiny*.

Pocketing the compass, Tom drew his sword. Its blade reflected the red sky, flashing like a tongue of fire as he approached the courtyard. He lifted his shield, preparing to do battle. Then he stepped out into the open, his boots ringing on the cobbles. Elenna was at his shoulder, an arrow poised on her bow, her eyes gleaming.

"Keep me covered," Tom said to her. "But don't put yourself in danger."

He moved into the centre of the courtyard, keeping his eyes fixed on the prowling Beast. Kaymon paced back and forth, her feet thumping and her claws rattling on the stones. The evil Beast's yellow eyes were filled with malice.

Lifting his sword, Tom closed in.

Kaymon paused, her throat rumbling with a low, menacing growl.

"This is for Silver!" Tom shouted as he rushed towards the Beast.

Kaymon crouched low, snarling as Tom came at her. Then she flexed her mighty leg muscles and leaped right over Tom's head! He thrust his sword up high, slicing the air, but the Beast was out of range.

Tom turned swiftly, his shield up and his sword ready.

Kaymon landed on the stone steps that led to the battlements. Howling, the Beast leaped again, high above Tom's head. But this time, in the middle of the leap, her shape swelled – and suddenly there were three hounds in the air.

They separated and came crashing down onto the cobbles with a noise like an avalanche. Tom spun round. The three hounds had surrounded him, their eyes burning with sinister satisfaction as they moved slowly forwards, their menacing growls filling the courtyard. Tom turned, trying desperately to keep all three Beasts at bay with his flashing sword. But as he turned to confront two of the hounds, the third leaped forwards behind him, one great paw reaching out, claws gleaming.

Using the power given to him by the golden boots, Tom sprang over the hound's head. Jaws snapped at his heels as he soared through the air. He twisted in mid-leap, his feet striking high on the courtyard wall. He bent his knees on impact and kicked out, the force sending him flying across the courtyard above the howling Beasts.

"For Avantia!" he shouted, striking down at them with his sword as he sped over their heads.

"Well done!" Elenna called.

Tom felt full of energy and power as he landed on the cobbles, the golden chainmail giving him extra strength of heart in battle. The hounds pounced, but before they

were able to sink their fangs into
him, he leaped up high again,
turning a somersault in midair.

One hound jumped up, razor-sharp
claws raking and teeth gnashing. Tom
stamped hard on the hound's muzzle,
bounding high again and back-
flipping before he came plunging
down to the ground.

The hounds howled with rage. Tom watched as they came for him. He intended to make another leap, hoping they would crash into one another. But he left his jump a moment too late.

One of the hounds reached out with a great paw, and its curled yellow claws struck Tom on the wrist, knocking his sword out of his hand. The steel blade clattered as it hit the cobbles. The hound's paw reached out again, the dreadful claws catching the sword and sending it skimming across the courtyard, out of Tom's reach.

Ignoring the pain in his wrist, Tom gripped his shield and watched the three hounds pad relentlessly towards him.

They were unstoppable!

He braced himself as the Beasts
lunged forwards, their teeth dripping
saliva and their twisted claws slashing
at him. Would he survive?

CHAPTER EIGHT

BRAINS AGAINST BRAWN

The three hounds pounced as one. But Tom sprang straight up into the air, and the Beasts crashed together, howling and yelping.

Tom plunged downwards, landing with all his weight on the huge head of one of the hounds. He used it as a springboard, leaping sideways this time, and cartwheeling over the hound's back.

He landed hard, skidding across the cobbles, using his shield to protect himself from injury. Then he retrieved his sword and crouched with his back to the wall, ready for the next attack.

The three hounds turned to him, their eyes brimming with hatred, and their hair bristling like wire along their backs.

While there's blood in my veins, Tom thought, *it is my destiny to confront these evil creatures – and defeat them*.

But it was still three against one! For every set of deadly fangs Tom avoided, two more were ready to take their place.

An arrow flew from Elenna's bow. It skipped on the cobbles close to the front paw of one hound. The Beast turned, its eyes fixed on Elenna, its jaws slavering.

Tom had to stop the hounds from attacking his friend! *I must trap them*, he thought. He dashed along the wall and bounded through an open doorway. Then he slammed the door shut, hammering home the bolt before racing across the room and leaping through another door, which led into a long corridor.

Glancing back, he saw the hounds smash open the first door. They fought and struggled to get in through the entrance. At last, they forced their way into the room, snarling and biting at one another.

Tom's plan was working. In the narrow confines of the castle, there wasn't room for three massive hounds.

Tom could see Elenna beyond the doorway. "Shoot at them!" he called.

"Don't let them out into the open again! I want them to chase me!"

"It's too dangerous for you!" Elenna shouted.

"No, it isn't!" Tom yelled back. "If they want to catch me inside, they'll have to change back to single form. Then I have more chance of winning!"

Moments, later, an arrow sped in through the doorway, grazing the flank of one of the hounds. *Well done, Elenna!* Tom thought.

He raced along the corridor, looking over his shoulder. Driven on by Elenna's arrows, the three hounds all tried to push through the second doorway. They were snapping and growling and thrashing about as each tried to get into the corridor ahead of the others.

"Come and get me!" Tom shouted.
"If you can!"

The three mouths opened wide
in howls of rage and frustration,
the dreadful din echoing along
the corridor. Tom laughed as the
creatures merged together once
more. He'd done it!

A moment later, one huge Kaymon
came thundering down the corridor

with death in her eyes. Tom noticed that the Beast was panting heavily, her chest heaving as though her heart were pounding fit to burst. Thick saliva drooled from her fangs and her twisted claws scratched deep grooves in the stonework as she tore forwards.

Tom swept the tapestry aside and ran down into the dungeons. His heart hammering, he slipped into the shadows at the foot of the winding staircase. With a howl, Kaymon came hurtling down in pursuit. As the Beast passed him, Tom dodged back up the stairs. Kaymon turned at the sound of his footsteps, but lost her balance and tumbled over. She got up slowly, panting hard, her chest rising and falling rapidly. She was tiring, her body too huge for all this chasing.

As Tom ran into the corridor again, he heard claws scrabbling on the stone staircase behind him. This was not going to be easy! He raced along the corridor and stumbled back into the first room.

Elenna was there, an arrow fixed to her bow.

"Keep out of sight," Tom gasped as he ran past her. "Let her pass you. Shoot at her from behind if she looks like giving chase. She's tiring. I think her heart could give out!"

"Good luck!" Elenna said.

Tom headed out into the courtyard and made for the steps that led to the battlements.

As he arrived at the top, he saw Kaymon on the bottom of the steps. The great Beast was clearly in trouble – her mouth hung open and her red tongue lolled. There were flecks of foam at her lips.

"Come on!" Tom taunted. "Don't give up now!"

Kaymon let out a howl that made the stones under Tom's feet tremble. Gathering all her remaining strength, the Beast mounted the stairs in three leaps. Tom ran as fast as he could. Elenna was down in the courtyard, firing arrows that bounced on the stones, narrowly missing the gasping Beast as she came careering along the battlements towards Tom.

Tom raced to the gatehouse and leaped onto it. He stared down at the drawbridge that spanned the weed-choked moat and looked back over his shoulder – Kaymon was still chasing him, her body heaving and her breath ragged. Tom jumped from

the battlements. He knew that the
eagle's feather embedded in his
shield, which came from Arcta the
mountain giant, would protect him
from the fall.

As he dropped through the air, he could hear Elenna shouting encouragement from the courtyard.

He came thudding down onto the rotting timbers of the drawbridge. They groaned beneath his weight. He ran to the far end and looked up, his sword at the ready.

Kaymon was on top of the battlements, roaring as she stared down at him.

"Follow me, if you can!" Tom shouted. "Or are you too tired?"

With a ferocious snarl, Kaymon leaped off the castle walls. She plunged down towards the drawbridge, roaring and slavering.

Her tremendous weight landed heavily on the rotten wood. With a crack, the bridge collapsed. A long splinter flew through the air

towards Tom. He ducked, but its
sharp edges grazed his cheek,
drawing blood.

The massive hound fell into
the moat, sending up a torrent of
slimy green water. Tom stood at the
edge, watching as the evil Beast
floundered, gasping and straining
to keep her head above the foul
waters.

He felt a moment of pity, but it
passed. Kaymon was nothing but evil.

Elenna appeared at the gateway.
Carefully avoiding the hole in the
drawbridge, she ran over to Tom.

The light was fading from the
Beast's wicked eyes as the weeds
tangled around her body, pulling her
down. As the huge head slipped
under the thrashing water for the
final time, Tom saw the waters begin
to spin, as if being stirred by an
invisible stick.

Faster and faster the whirlpool

spun, and then a hole opened up at its centre.

"Look!" cried Elenna, pointing to the blue sky and snow-clad mountains that had appeared at the bottom of the hole. "It's Avantia! We'll be able to get Nanook home!"

A sudden fear filled Tom's heart. The gateway to Avantia would only stay with them for a few precious moments.

Where was Nanook?

CHAPTER NINE
SHADOW PLAY

Tom turned at the sound of huge feet beating a path across the moor.

"Nanook!" he shouted in relief, seeing the great shaggy snow monster racing towards them. Storm was galloping in her wake.

"Here she comes!" Elenna cried. "And she's carrying Silver!"

Tom saw the limp shape of the wolf in Nanook's arms. "She must have understood that it was time to find us," Tom said.

The good Beast came to a halt and crouched so that Elenna could examine Silver. The wolf was weak but still alive, and he even managed to lick Elenna's hand as she leaned anxiously over him.

"The wounds are all healed," Elenna said, checking Silver's fur. "But I think he's still exhausted from the ordeal. He can't even stand."

Nanook looked at Tom with her huge, kind eyes and snorted softly.

"She wants to take Silver back to Avantia so he can get well again," Tom said, grateful once more to the red jewel in his belt, which allowed him to understand Nanook.

"Yes," Elenna said. "That's a good idea." She threw her arms around

Silver's neck. "We'll see you very soon," she said, hiding her face in his thick grey fur.

Tom looked down into the moat. The whirling water was beginning to slow and the gateway was shrinking. Soon it would be gone and Nanook would be trapped here.

"Elenna!" Tom urged gently. "We don't have much time!"

Elenna stepped back. "No, of course," she said, wiping her sleeve across her eyes.

"Nanook!" Tom called. "Jump!"

Still cradling the injured wolf in her arms, the snow monster lumbered to the edge of the moat. She looked over her shoulder, grunting her thanks, then she leaped into the gateway.

The water churned as she disappeared, then stilled, leaving only slowly spreading ripples.

"I hope he'll be safe," Elenna murmured, staring down into the water.

Tom rested his hand on her shoulder. "I'm sure he will," he said. "Aduro will make him fit and well again in no time. You'll see."

Storm thrust his head between

them, nuzzling up against Elenna's face.

"I missed you, boy!" Tom said, stroking the stallion's long nose and patting his neck. "You did well, helping Nanook to look after Silver. But I have another job for you, Storm. You'll have to take us to our next Quest. I'm sure Aduro will soon tell us what it is."

Just then something caught Tom's attention: a bright glint that shone up from the surface of the moat, close to where he had last seen Kaymon.

"What's that?" he asked, walking to the water's edge.

"It's the white jewel from Kaymon's collar," Elenna said.

"Yes, it is!" said Tom. "I think I can reach it." He crouched, leaning out over the stagnant water, while

Elenna held onto his belt to stop him
from falling.

The jewel was just out of reach. He
drew his sword and with the point
gently edged it towards himself. At
last he was able to pick it up. He
rubbed it on his tunic, cleaning off
the slime.

"Another jewel for my belt!" he
said. "I wonder what it will do?"

"Fit it in place and we'll soon find
out," Elenna urged him.

Tom slotted the gemstone in place.

"Well?" Elenna asked. "Do you feel anything?"

Tom shook his head. "I feel exactly the same," he said.

A few moments passed and Tom was just beginning to wonder if anything would happen at all, when the jewel let out a single blinding pulse of white light.

Tom rubbed his eyes. "What just happened?" he gasped.

He blinked a couple of times to clear his vision, and when he looked at Elenna she was staring open-mouthed at something behind his back.

He turned. The high sun cast his shadow at his feet. But something odd was happening – the shadow was moving on its own. As Tom stood

gazing down at it, the shadow picked itself up out of the grass and stood in front of him with its hands on its hips, its head turning slowly.

"Er...hello there..." Tom ventured.

The shadow jumped back, as if startled to hear Tom's voice. Then it doubled over, its hands on its knees.

"He's laughing!" Elenna gasped.

The shadow straightened up again and ran lightly towards the moor.

Tom grinned. "Thanks to Kaymon, I think we have another companion on our Quest!"

The shadow leaped into the air, soundlessly clapping its hands. As it ran ahead Tom watched, laughing. With their new friend, they'd be more than ready for Malvel's next challenge.

Join Tom on the next stage
of the Beast Quest

Meet

TusK
THE MIGHTY
MAMMOTH

Can Tom free the good Beasts from
the Dark Realm?

PROLOGUE

"Feel my blade!" Marco slashed and stabbed with his wooden sword, made from a tree branch. "There! I have defeated another enemy of the Gorgon rebels!"

His mother's voice rang out from the nearby settlement. "Marco! Get back on watch!"

With a sigh, Marco crammed his sword into his belt and climbed back up the lookout tree, an oak that stood at the edge of the forest. From its branches he could peer down on the small rebel camp where he lived and see right across the forest, all the way to the northern hills.

The rebel camp was in a heavily forested part of Gorgonia. The leaders of the rebellion came here to make plans for the overthrow of Malvel, the Dark Wizard.

Marco's job was very important. If he spotted any Gorgonian guards, his task was to run and warn the Seniors – the men and women who governed the camp. The rebels' weapons would be thrown into a pit and covered with leafy branches, while the leaders would quickly disguise themselves as ordinary hunters and traders.

Marco shifted in his perch. He pulled his tunic close about his neck to ward off the cold wind. A movement on a far hilltop caught his eye. He peered into the distance, but couldn't quite make out what it was. He climbed higher, then gave a gasp of amazement and delight.

It was a huge creature, covered with scales that shimmered. Vast leathery wings stretched wide, jet-black against the red Gorgonian sky. Puffs of white smoke came from its nostrils.

"A dragon!" Marco murmured. He had never seen a dragon before, but he loved the stories he had been told of the beautiful, legendary Beasts – and the creature that stood on the far hilltop was most definitely a dragon!

"It's amazing!" Marco said. But where had it come from? There were no dragons in Gorgonia.

He had to let the Seniors know what he had seen. He was about to clamber down the tree when he spotted a disturbance on the far edge of the forest. Trees waved and shuddered, as though something huge were pushing through them.

As he watched, a gigantic creature came stamping out of the forest. It was a mammoth as large as a moving house, its back covered in thick brown hair that hung in shaggy tangles to its feet. The mammoth lifted her head, sending her trunk writhing up into the sky as she let out a deep battle cry.

Then she thundered up the hillside towards the dragon. Marco could see scars and old wounds on the mammoth's ears – but what he especially noticed were her long, curved tusks. As she charged, they sparkled and glinted like gold.

The dragon turned, lifting its head. Then it opened its wings, preparing to take to the air. But it was too late. Her head down, the mammoth crashed into the dragon's scaly side. She jerked her head up, catching the dragon with her long tusks, heaving the startled Beast onto its side. Marco watched in dismay as the mammoth wrapped her strong trunk around the dragon's neck and dragged the helpless creature into the forest.

"Let it go!" Marco shouted.

The mammoth's head lifted sharply. Marco gave a gasp of alarm. The monster had heard him! Small, red eyes peered across the forest, filled with anger and evil. Then the Beast charged through the trees, pushing them aside as she headed straight for Marco.

The oak shook as the evil mammoth huge head hammered into its trunk. There was a tearing noise as the deep roots were wrenched out of the ground. The tree began to tilt at a dangerous angle. Marco lost his footing and hung on with his arms.

But the Beast had struck the tree with such force that her golden tusks had become embedded in the trunk. She twisted her head, trying to pull herself free. A thick, clear liquid was oozing from her tusks and dripping down from the tree. It gave off a terrible, toxic stench.

The tree was now at such an angle that Marco could let go and drop safely to the ground.

Picking himself up, he raced back to the village.

But as he ran, he saw something else that made his heart thud. Marching along the track was a company of Gorgonian guards...

CHAPTER ONE

TO THE RESCUE!

"Tom!" Elenna called with a smile.
"If you don't stop playing with your new
friend, we'll never get started on our Quest."

Tom grinned back at her. "You'd be the
same if your shadow suddenly came to life!"
he said, watching the fleeting black shape as
it vanished around a corner of the castle.

His shadow had leapt into action the
moment Tom had fitted Kaymon the gorgon
hound's white jewel into his magic belt.

Tom's vision blurred, then he suddenly
realised that he could see two different
viewpoints at the same time. With his own
eyes, he could see the wall of the castle, but
he could also see through his shadow's eyes.
He was able to scan the land of Gorgornia,
stretching away behind the castle.

"So that's my latest magic skill!" Tom
gasped. "I'll be able to send my shadow ahead
to check for danger. Hey!" he called. "Come

back here, please!"

The shadow bounded back around the corner and skidded to a halt at his feet.

"You're going to make a useful addition to the team!" Tom laughed, as his shadow reattached itself to him. He turned and walked back to where Elenna and his stallion, Storm, were waiting.

Elenna looked questioningly at him. "Do you know where our next Quest will take us?"

Before Tom could reply, the air between them began to ripple like water. Light blazed for a moment and then an image of their friend, the good wizard Aduro, appeared in front of them.

"Is Silver with you?" Elenna asked anxiously. Her wolf had been badly hurt in their last Quest, and Nanook the snow monster had taken him through the gateway into Avantia to be healed.

"He is quite safe," Aduro reassured her. "He is being well looked after. But a new evil Beast awaits you. She is a formidable foe. Her name is Tusk."

"Is she a mammoth?" Tom asked. He had seen the great shaggy animals occasionally in Avantia.

"Yes," Aduro said. "But a mammoth unlike any you have ever imagined."

"What do you mean?" asked Elenna.

The air began to ripple again, and the image of the good wizard flickered and trembled. "Alas, I must go," he called, his voice fading. "My magic is weakening. Good luck, my friends – and be careful. You are going into greater danger than you suspect."

The image disappeared.

Tom's heart sank. These brief visits from Aduro always reminded him of how far he was from home. Then he shook himself. There's no time to waste, he thought. A new Quest was waiting for them!

"At least I know Silver is all right," Elenna said. "Do you think the Gorgonian map will show us where we have to go?"

"I hope so," Tom said. He felt a vibration in his shield. He looked at the six tokens, given to him by the good Beasts of Avantia, that were embedded in it. The scale of Ferno the fire dragon was glowing red.

"Ferno is in danger!" Tom said. He took out the map that Malvel had given them. They were never sure if it would show them a true path or lead them into deadly peril – but it was the only guide they had.

Spreading out the map, Tom saw a small image of the fire dragon in a region of thick forest.

"That's no more than a day's ride north," Elenna said. She pointed to a red circle drawn on the map at the southern edge of the forest. "And it's close to the rebel camp that Odora marked for us."

"Yes," Tom agreed, remembering the rebel girl who had aided them in their Quest to defeat Narga the sea monster. "That's the one thing on this map we know we can trust!" He leapt into Storm's saddle. "Come on. We have another good Beast to rescue!"

Elenna sprang up behind him.
With a loud neigh, Storm set off at a gallop.

"We'll have to pass close to the rebel camp," Elenna said. "Do you think we should stop there for food and water?"

"That's a good idea," Tom said.

Soon they were moving through a land of rolling hills and forested valleys. Tom looked at his shield. The dragon scale was glowing more darkly now. He had a sense of foreboding as Storm galloped on beneath the red Gorgonian sky. Suddenly his mind was filled with a dark vision of Ferno writhing and crying out in pain.

"Hurry, boy!" Tom urged.

"What's wrong?" Elenna asked, clinging on as the stallion went even faster.

"I don't think Ferno has long to live," Tom called over his shoulder. He couldn't keep the concern out of his voice. "I hope we get to him in time!"

Could their Quest be over before it began?

Follow this Quest to the end in TUSK THE MIGHTY MAMMOTH.

Win an exclusive
Beast Quest T-shirt and goody bag!

In every Beast Quest book the Beast Quest logo is hidden
in one of the pictures. Find the logos in book 13 to book
18 and make a note of which pages they appear on.
Send the six page numbers to us. Each month we will
draw one winner to receive a Beast Quest T-shirt
and goody bag.

Send your entry on a postcard listing
the title of this book and the winning
page number to:

THE BEAST QUEST COMPETITION:
KAYMON THE GORGON HOUND
Orchard Books
338 Euston Road, London NW1 3BH
Australian readers should email:
childrens.books@hachette.com.au

New Zealand readers should write to:
Beast Quest Competition
4 Whetu Place, Mairangi Bay, Auckland, NZ
or email: childrensbooks@hachette.co.nz

Only one entry per child.
Final draw: 31 October 2009

You can also enter this competition
via the Beast Quest website: www.beastquest.co.uk

Fight the Beasts,
Fear the Magic

www.beastquest.co.uk

Have you checked out the all-new Beast Quest website?
It's the place to go for games, downloads, activities,
sneak previews and lots of fun!

You can read all about your favourite Beast Quest
monsters, download free screensavers and desktop
wallpapers for your computer, and send
beastly e-cards to your friends.

Sign up to the newsletter at www.beastquest.co.uk
to receive exclusive extra content and the opportunity
to enter special members-only competitions. It's the best
place to go for up-to-date info on all the Beast Quest
books, including the next exciting series,
which features six brand new Beasts.

Series 1

Ferno the Fire Dragon	978 1 84616 483 5
Sepron the Sea Serpent	978 1 84616 482 8
Arcta the Mountain Giant	978 1 84616 484 2
Tagus the Horse-Man	978 1 84616 486 6
Nanook the Snow Monster	978 1 84616 485 9
Epos the Flame Bird	978 1 84616 487 3

Vedra & Krimon: Twin Beasts of Avantia	978 1 84616 951 9

Series 2: The Golden Armour

Zepha the Monster Squid	978 1 84616 988 5
Claw the Giant Monkey	978 1 84616 989 2
Soltra the Stone Charmer	978 1 84616 990 8
Vipero the Snake Man	978 1 84616 991 5
Arachnid the King of Spiders	978 1 84616 992 2
Trillion the Three-Headed Lion	978 1 84616 993 9

Spiros the Ghost Phoenix	978 1 84616 994 6

Series 3: The Dark Realm

Torgor the Minotaur	978 1 84616 997 7
Skor the Winged Stallion	978 1 84616 998 4
Narga the Sea Monster	978 1 40830 000 8
Kaymon the Gorgon Hound	978 1 40830 001 5
Tusk the Mighty Mammoth	978 1 40830 002 2
Sting the Scorpion Man	978 1 40830 003 9

All priced at £4.99

Vedra & Krimon: Twin Beasts of Avantia and *Spiros the Ghost Phoenix* are priced at £5.99

The Beast Quest books are available from all good
bookshops, or can be ordered direct from the publisher:
Orchard Books, PO BOX 29, Douglas IM99 1BQ.
Credit card orders please telephone 01624 836000
or fax 01624 837033 or visit our website: www.orchardbooks.co.uk
or e-mail: bookshop@enterprise.net for details.

To order please quote title, author
and ISBN and your full name and address.
Cheques and postal orders should be made payable to 'Bookpost plc.'
Postage and packing is FREE within the UK
(overseas customers should add £2.00 per book).

Prices and availability are subject to change.